D1541577

TEACHER TROUBLE

and other short stories

by Dianne Swenson

Illustrations: Douglas M. Rife

CONTENTS

TEACHER
TROUBLE

Mr. Graves was the new English teacher. He always seemed to pick on Kip.

"Why didn't you turn in your work?" Mr. Graves asked Kip one day.

Kip told him he was too busy. Then Mr. Graves got mad. He made Kip stay after school.

Mr. Graves should have known better. Kip was a leader. His friends were tough. They ran the school. Other kids did what Kip's crowd wanted or else they paid the consequences.

Kip didn't pick fights. Kip hardly ever had to fight. His friends fought for him.

This attitude was the same in class. Kip's crowd liked some teachers. Then they behaved. But they didn't like other teachers. Kip and his friends made trouble for those teachers.

They talked in class. They threw things. They talked back to the teacher.

Teachers who got in Kip's way tried to put up with him for a while. But they always learned the hard way. Sometimes they even quit teaching. The teachers said they couldn't handle the kids anymore.

One teacher thought she could change Kip. She helped Kip with his work. She was nice to him.

So Kip asked her to go out with him. He thought she liked him. He didn't know she just wanted to help him with his school work.

The teacher tried to explain to Kip

why she couldn't go out with him. But the more she talked, the madder Kip got. He told her off.

Kip thought he could go out with any girl he wanted. He didn't understand how anyone could turn him down.

Kip scared her. He said he could make her life hard. His friends would help. He just had to give the word.

The teacher never came back. She got sick. Some of the kids felt bad. They knew she only wanted to help Kip. She just didn't know how to do it.

Then Mr. Graves came. He was hard on Kip.

"We all have to do our work. Even you, Kip," Mr. Graves told him. Kip had to stay after school.

"We all have to come to class on time. Even you, Kip," Mr. Graves told Kip when he was late. He made him stay after school again.

"We all had to write this paper. Even you, Kip," Mr. Graves said. Kip didn't turn a paper in. He had to stay after school all week.

That was more than Kip could stand. He was mad. He told his friends. They did the rest.

They got everybody in class to talk. The kids threw spitballs and paper airplanes. Everyone goofed off all hour.

Mr. Graves told the kids to stop. But nobody did. So Mr. Graves just let them all goof off.

At the end of class he said, "You all owe me an hour. You wasted an hour of class. You can make it up after school. Anyone who doesn't show up has to do double time. I'll call your parents today. I'll tell them you'll be late."

The kids thought he was bluffing. No

one showed up after school. But when the kids got home, their parents were waiting for them.

The next day, the kids talked during Mr. Graves' class again. At the end he said, "You now have three hours to make up. Two for yesterday, one for today."

"You'd better come tonight," he said. "If you don't, you can't come back to school. Not unless your parents come with you."

No one showed up again. The kids thought Mr. Graves was trying to scare them. They didn't think he was serious. But he was. He didn't let anyone back into his class. Not until their parents came. He called every parent to tell them what he was doing.

After that, the kids cooled it for a while. They didn't want their parents

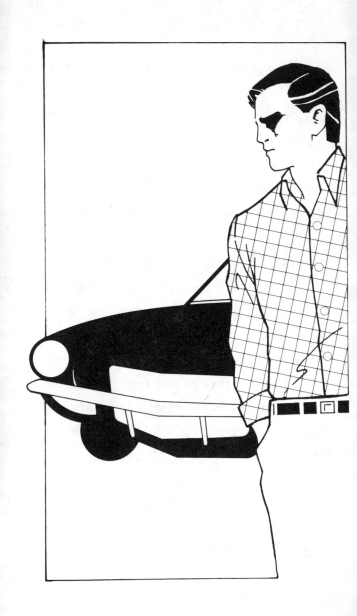

mad at them. But Kip was still mad at Mr. Graves.

Kip found out where Mr. Graves lived. His car was always parked in front of his house. Kip had an idea.

Kip wanted to be in on the action this time. He didn't want his friends to do it all for him. He led the whole plan.

After dark, Kip and his friends slashed the tires on Mr. Graves' car. They didn't make any noise. Nobody heard them.

They thought Mr. Graves wouldn't be in school the next day. They thought he'd be too scared to come. They thought he'd have to take the day off to get new tires.

But Mr. Graves was there. Another teacher gave him a ride.

"I'm very upset that someone slashed my tires last night. I'm afraid it was a student," Mr. Graves said when class began. "I don't know why someone would do that. I hope someone will help me. Please tell me who did it. I'm sure someone knows."

The kids did know who it was. But they were afraid to tell Mr. Graves. Some of the kids thought Kip was wrong. But they were scared to say anything to Mr. Graves. They would get in trouble themselves.

Nobody talked. Every day Mr. Graves asked them to speak up.

"You all know it was wrong," he said. "Even the people who did it. Let's get this thing out in the open."

But nobody told him anything. Kip went around bragging to all the kids.

A few nights later, Kip and his friends threw a rock at Mr. Graves' house. They broke a window. They got away before the police came.

The next day in school, Mr. Graves asked if anyone knew who broke his window.

"My wife and baby son were in that room. They could have been hurt. It's one thing to destroy my tires. It's something else to hurt people I love."

Mr. Graves stopped and looked around the room. "Who is upset with me?" he asked. "Please tell me. You don't have to speak up now. Just see me after class or after school. We can work this out."

Some of the kids thought Kip should tell. Kip just laughed at them.

"No way. And you'd better not say anything yourself," Kip told them.

A few of the kids talked about telling Mr. Graves. But it got back to Kip. He told them he would beat them up. That ended all the talk.

Before long, the quarter was almost over. Kip was still giving Mr. Graves a hard time. He didn't turn in his work. He never wrote any of his papers.

Mr. Graves made Kip stay after school. That didn't matter. Kip still didn't work. He was flunking all of his tests.

"He'll never flunk me," Kip said. "I've done worse than this in other classes. The teachers are afraid to flunk me. They know what I'll do to them."

But Mr. Graves didn't act like any of the other teachers. He flunked Kip.

Nobody ever saw Kip so mad. He tore his report card up.

"I'm going to get that guy," he said. "He'll never come back to this school again."

Kip wrote Mr. Graves a note. It said,

Watch your step—or else!

That afternoon Mr. Graves walked into the room. "I got a note in my office mailbox today," Mr. Graves told the class. "Someone threatened me."

The class was silent. Mr. Graves went on. "I know that living in the city isn't always safe. But I took this job because I knew I could do it. It's a tough job. A lot of teachers don't want it. But I love it."

"Lately things haven't gone so well," he added. "My tires were slashed. My window was broken." Mr. Graves looked at the class. Some of the kids wouldn't look at him.

"But I'm going to stay." Mr. Graves told the class. "You're learning something. For some of you, it's the first time you've learned anything. A lot of you are smarter than you thought."

Mr. Graves looked right at Kip. "But some of you aren't learning. You have to work or you won't get by. That's not just in class. It's like that in life. If you don't do the work, you won't keep the job. Your job here is to do your school work."

Kip looked right back at Mr. Graves. Kip didn't say a word. But his face got red. He looked mad.

Kip wanted to get back at the teacher. He decided to do something awful to Mr. Graves. Kip knew how the teacher felt about his wife and his son. He knew Mr. Graves cared about his family.

So Kip sent a note to Mrs. Graves. He told her to make her husband quit his job. If she didn't, her baby would be gone.

Kip bragged about what he had done. "I'm going to get rid of Graves for good," he said.

The next day Mr. Graves came into the room. His face looked awful. Everyone knew his wife had read Kip's note.

"My wife received an awful note yesterday. Whoever sent it said they would hurt our baby," Mr. Graves told the class. His eyes looked sad.

"I've done all I can to help you kids," he said. "I've made you do your work. You know you can do it well. Many of you have begun to do well. I'm proud of you.

"But it only takes one person to ruin everything. My wife wants us to move away from this city right away. She's already left with the baby. I can't tell you where she is. We're both afraid someone might try to follow them."

He stopped talking. He looked at

everyone. Kip looked right back at him. But most of the kids couldn't look at Mr. Graves. They felt awful. They knew they should tell.

"I'll give you a week," Mr. Graves said. "Tell me who wrote the note by next Tuesday. Then I'll stay. Otherwise, I'll leave. The safety of my family comes first."

He smiled sadly. "I'll feel bad if I have to quit this job," he said. "I want to stay. I just hope some of you want me to stay, too."

After class, the kids talked about what Mr. Graves had said. They were still afraid of Kip. But even some of Kip's best friends were upset. They didn't like the way things had turned out.

The days passed. Nothing happened. Each day, Mr. Graves looked a little sadder.

At last, Tuesday came. "This is my last day of class," Mr. Graves said. "You'll have a new teacher tomorrow. I hope your new teacher can help you. I've tried. But I've failed."

"You haven't failed." A boy in the back of the room spoke up. All eyes turned to look at him. It was Phil Kane. Phil was a good friend of Kip's.

"We're the ones who have failed," Phil said. "We were too afraid to tell you what we know. We do know who did those awful things to you. I even helped slash your tires and break your window. I'm willing to pay for the damages. I never knew things would go this far. I was wrong."

Mr. Graves smiled. "Thank you, Phil. I know how you feel about being afraid. But you should get rid of your fear. Get it out in the open. Don't let one person control your life. If you do, you'll never be free."

Mr. Graves worked hard to keep the class going for the rest of the hour. But no one could work. The kids knew that Mr. Graves was a good teacher. They wanted him to stay. But they were still too afraid to talk.

At the end of the hour, Phil stopped Kip in the hall. "Listen to me, Kip. Tell Mr. Graves what you've done. If you don't, I will."

"You wouldn't dare," Kip told him.

"Oh, yes I would. I'm not afraid of you anymore," Phil said.

A bunch of kids had gathered around. "We'll go with you," said one of Phil's friends. He had helped slash Mr. Graves' tires, too.

By this time the whole class was around Kip and Phil.

"I'll kill you all if you do," Kip yelled.

"No you won't," Phil told him. "We've done your dirty work. But things have gone too far this time. Now you get in there right now, or we will. We're sick of you bullying everyone. Right?"

Kip looked around. Heads were nodding. People were saying, "Right."

Kip couldn't see how everyone could turn against him. But no one was on his side, now.

"What will it be?" Phil asked him. "Do we go in and tell Mr. Graves? Or do you? I hope you'll go in yourself. Act like you're sorry. It'll be better for you. Maybe Mr. Graves won't call the police."

"Will you go in with me?" Kip asked Phil.

"Sure," Phil told him.

They walked back into the classroom. The kids all cheered. They knew it wasn't easy for Kip to go face Mr. Graves. But they were all glad he did.

Kip heard the cheers. He stopped at Mr. Graves' door. In a way, he was glad it was over. Mr. Graves couldn't be pushed around. Maybe he wasn't such a creep after all. Maybe learning wouldn't be so bad.

Kip took a deep breath and opened the door.

THE STRANGE GIRL

Jane did not get along with anyone at school. She had trouble with her teachers. None of her classmates liked her.

Jane didn't seem to care about other people. If someone acted nice to her, Jane didn't know what to do. She usually decided to be mean to them. She just didn't know how to make a friend. Even if she had friends, she wouldn't be able to keep them for long.

She had been a loner ever since grade school. Getting older hadn't changed her at all.

Jane took a reading class her

sophomore year. Her teacher was Miss Austin. At the beginning of the semester, Miss Austin divided her students into groups. Everyone had been in the same group all term except Jane. She had been moved from group to group. No one wanted to work with Jane.

Jane did strange things when she worked with others. Sometimes she would not say a word for the whole hour. Sometimes she talked loudly when everyone else was working. The worst times were when she would get upset for no reason. Then she would take someone's pencil or pen and throw it. Sometimes she would shout at the others in the group.

Jane had been in every group in Miss Austin's class. She never lasted more than a few days with any group. One day before Jane came into the room, Miss Austin told Sandy that Jane would be in her group.

"Oh, Miss Austin," Sandy said. "When Jane was in our group the last time, we didn't get anything done."

"I talked with Jane," Miss Austin explained. "She said she would try hard to work with you today."

"Well, I guess it's okay then," Sandy said.

"No, it isn't okay," said Jim, a boy in the group. "I don't want her in this group."

"I'm with Jim," said Sue, another girl in the group. "Why does she have to be with us? Why can't she work by herself?"

Miss Austin surveyed the class. "You are doing a group project," she said. "Jane needs to learn to work with others."

Dave was another boy in the group. "If she won't work with us, will you put her in another group?" he asked.

"Yes," Miss Austin said. "I told Jane that if she won't work with you, she will have to be moved or work alone. She does not want to do that. I think she will try harder today."

"I hope so," Jim said.

Just then Jane came in. The group started working. Jane sat down quietly. Soon she began tapping on her desk with a pencil. Then she reached over and grabbed Sue's pen. She dropped it on the floor and laughed. Next Jane took Jim's paper. She wadded it up and threw it.

"Stop bugging me, you creep," Jim said.

"You can't make me," Jane shouted at him.

"Give my pen back," Sue said.

"Pick it up yourself!"

Dave had been watching Jane cause trouble. Everybody usually listened to him.

"Cut out the yelling," he said. "We have to get the first part of this story done today."

"I don't want to do this stupid story," Jane said.

"You told Miss Austin you would work with us," Sandy said.

"I did not!"

"Yes you did," Sandy replied. "Miss Austin said you did."

Before anyone else could say anything, Jane stood up. She tipped her desk over. Then she grabbed Sandy's purse. She ran quickly out of the room.

Miss Austin asked Sandy to go to the office and report what Jane had done.

Nobody in Sue's group could work. They were mad at Jane. They talked about how awful she was. None of them wanted to work with her again.

"Okay, everyone. Settle down," Miss Austin said. The students stopped talking.

"Thank you. I think we should talk about Jane's problem," Miss Austin told them.

"I think she should be kicked out," Jim said. "You wouldn't let any of us get away with the things she does."

"Yes," Sue said. "Jane gets away with murder."

"I understand how you feel," Miss Austin said. "But you know that Jane needs your understanding."

"We try," Dave told her. "But she almost makes it impossible."

Jim nodded. "We can't get anything

done with her in our group."

"Why can't she go to another group?"
Sue asked.

Miss Austin looked at each person in
the group. They knew she cared about
what they had to say.

"I put her in your group because you
four would at least try to get along with
her," she said. "I know how hard it is.
You see, Jane can't tell the difference
between someone who wants to be her
friend and someone who doesn't. I think
she feels everyone is out to get her. She
needs your help. You will just have to
keep on trying."

"Why should we try to help her?" Jim
asked.

Sue nodded. "Yes. Why should we?"
she asked.

Before Miss Austin could say
anything, Sandy rushed into the room.

"Miss Austin!" Sandy yelled. "Jane climbed up the old fire escape on the side of the school! She won't come down!"

Miss Austin and her reading group rushed out to the side of the building. Jane had climbed to the platform at the top of the stairs. She stood close to the edge. She was holding onto the thin metal rail that ran around the platform.

As soon as Jane saw Miss Austin and the group she yelled, "Go away!"

"Jane, you must come down," Miss Austin said. "That old fire escape is dangerous. It hasn't been used for years."

"If you don't go away, I'm going to jump," Jane yelled.

"I wish she would," Sue told Jim.

"I don't know," Jim said. "She's up pretty high. She could be badly hurt."

"I don't know why she has to do these

things," Sue said.

Miss Austin heard what Sue said to Jim. "Do you see now how much Jane needs our help?" Miss Austin asked Sue.

"Yes. I didn't think she would do anything like this," Sue replied.

Sandy tried to talk Jane into coming down. "If you come down, I won't be mad at you for taking my purse," she called to Jane.

"Yes, you will," Jane shouted back at her.

"No, I won't!"

"I'm not coming down. You don't want me in your group. No one wants me!" she sobbed.

"Please come down," Dave called up at her.

"You all hate me!" Jane screamed.

"No we don't," Sandy told her. "We

just don't understand why you do the things you do."

"We didn't want you to run out of the room and climb up this fire escape," Dave added. "We don't want you to get hurt."

"See. You don't want me," Jane yelled.

"The group wants to help you," Miss Austin called to her. "But you must help yourself first. When you take things, you make others angry. You have to learn that people do care about you."

"But I can't do the work!" Jane cried.

"You can do it, Jane. The others are there to help you. That's what a group is for, right?" Miss Austin turned to look at the group.

"Yes," Dave and Sandy shouted. But nobody else spoke.

"Sue and Jim won't help me. They

hate me," Jane said. "I'm going to jump."

Jane took one hand off the bar. She lifted up one foot over the railing. The old iron stairway creaked loudly.

"No Jane! Don't jump!" Sue screamed.

"You told Jim you wanted me to jump," Jane shouted back at her.

"I didn't mean it," Sue shouted. "I was mad because you threw my pen on the floor. But I don't want you to hurt yourself."

"Jim wants me to jump," Jane insisted.

"No, Jane," Jim told her. "I don't want you to get hurt. Please come down."

"If I come down, you will just yell at me!"

"No, Jane," Miss Austin said. "We

won't yell at you."

Dave stepped forward. "Come down, Jane. I really want to help you. So does the rest of the group. We want you to be our friend."

Jane sat down on the platform. She set Sandy's purse down beside her. She put her head in her hands. Miss Austin and the others could her her crying.

"I'm going to climb up the stairs and talk to her," Dave told Miss Austin.

Dave climbed up the creaking stairs. He sat down beside Jane.

It's all right," he told her. "We meant it. We'll help you."

Jane looked at him through her tears. "Will you be my friend, too?" she asked softly.

"Yes," he said.

LOSING
CONTROL

I was in bad shape about a year ago. One day I almost made a big mistake. I almost lost control.

All I knew then was that I wanted to die. Life was a bore. Worse than that, life was a waste. I was a waste. I wasn't worth anything to anybody.

Even my parents didn't seem to care what happened to me. I felt like they wouldn't have cared if I had died. They had too many problems of their own.

My dad went from job to job. Most of the time, he was out of work. My mom was sick a lot. She was too sick to take care of me and my brothers and sisters.

My brothers and sisters and I had lived in a few different foster homes. Some of the homes had been okay. But usually they weren't any better than living with my parents. Some of my foster parents didn't like me any better than my mom or dad did.

I knew why they didn't like me. I didn't like myself. But I did like to cause trouble. I had made things rough for some of them. I had given them more problems than they could handle. I couldn't blame them for wanting to get rid of me.

I was back with my parents the day I almost lost control. They had wanted me back to help around the house.

They had wanted my money, too. I worked in an office two nights a week after school. I swept the floors and cleaned the bathrooms. It was a hard job.

I had wanted the job at first. The extra money had been great at the last foster home. The people in that home had been okay. They hadn't taken my money.

But then my parents got me back. They started taking my money away from me.

My mom and dad had somehow convinced the social worker that they could be good parents again. I still don't know how they managed to do that. My mom must have pretended she was feeling better. My dad had found another job at last. Somehow he had made the social worker think he could stick with that one.

Fat chance. How could the social worker be so dumb? Couldn't he see? All he had to do was look at my dad's record. It showed that he couldn't hold a job for more than a few months.

My dad worked for two weeks in his new job. Then he was fired again. Same old story. My dad was a loser.

But so what? I was a loser, too. My schoolwork had always been bad. I hated school. It was hard for me. The teachers never made it easy.

A few teachers had tried to help me. But I didn't believe that any of them ever really cared about me. It was all just part of the job.

Well, maybe Miss Winston had cared a little. But I had thought she would stop caring if I caused enough problems.

When I first met Miss Winston, she had just finished college. She acted like teaching kids was a big deal. At first I thought she was putting on a big act. After a while I knew Miss Winston thought she had a special job.

I did everything I could to show her how bad I could be. I didn't turn in my lessons. I skipped her classes. I was a real pain.

But Miss Winston kept telling me that I could learn. She kept telling me to apply myself. She said I could do great things if I wanted to.

I just laughed at her.

By the middle of the year, Miss Winston's eyelids drooped. She started to look like she hadn't slept for days.

One day a new teacher came to take her place. The new teacher told our class, "Miss Winston will be out for a few weeks."

The weeks turned into months. Miss Winston never came back. I heard from the other kids that she had had a nervous breakdown.

I thought about Miss Winston the

day I almost lost control. I decided that it was probably my fault that she had had a nervous breakdown. All the trouble I gave her had finally beaten her.

That day I decided that lots of things were my fault. It was probably my fault that my mother was sick so much. It must have been my fault that my dad couldn't keep a job. I hadn't been an easy kid to raise. My mother said that I cried all the time when I was a baby.

I was the fifth kid in my family. My mother told me that my dad had had a good job before I was born. He had worked for a long time building houses.

My dad had been laid off soon after I was born. He never got back on. After that, he went from job to job.

I came along at the wrong time. I was a problem from the start.

I thought of my brothers and sisters

that day, too. They weren't much better than I was. My oldest brother had been in trouble with the law. He was on probation for destroying some property My other brother had quit school at sixteen to get married. He already had a baby to take care of.

One of my sisters had followed my brother's example. She had dropped out of school at sixteen, too. She was living with some guy. Neither of them had jobs.

At least my other sister was a little better off than the rest of us. She had a decent job.

Maybe my brothers and one of my sisters were losers like my parents. But I was the worst of them all. I had been nothing but trouble for everybody.

That's what I thought the day I almost lost control. I thought that my family would be better off without me. My mom and dad were rid of everybody else. Everybody but me.

I wanted to make things easier for everyone. I had thought about it for a long time. I knew exactly how to do it.

I even had the gun. It was the same gun my older brother had used in a robbery. It had been easy to steal it from him. My stupid brother thought he had lost it.

I knew when I took the gun what I was going to do with it. I even kept it loaded all the time. I wanted it to be ready whenever I was.

I was ready that day. It would be easy. All I had to do was pull the trigger.

I was getting ready to do it when I heard a voice. "It wasn't your fault about Miss Winston," it told me. "Her boyfriend left her. That's why she had the breakdown. That's what everybody at school said."

The voice went on. "So what if your parents are losers? You don't have to be one, too. Look at your older sister. She made it. It wasn't easy for her, either."

I tried not to hear the voice. But it wouldn't go away.

"Your parents do love you. They have just had a hard time. And think about your girlfriend. Beth cares about you. Think how bad she would feel if you did something dumb, like kill yourself."

I thought about Beth. She was a great girl. I had been going out with her for a few months. She helped me with my schoolwork. I felt good when I was with her.

But Beth's parents didn't like me. They said I was a troublemaker. They

wanted Beth to stop seeing me. Pretty soon she would have to do what they wanted.

I decided that I might as well make it easy for her. I picked up the gun slowly.

I wondered if I should leave a note. What was the use? What would I say anyway? That nobody cared about me? That this was the best thing for everybody?

I could sense that the voice was about to come back and try to talk me out of it. The voice had always stopped me before.

I was going to beat the voice this time. But I couldn't pull the trigger fast enough.

A face flashed before me. It was the face of my friend, Joe. Joe had killed himself the year before.

"Don't do it," Joe said to me. "It isn't worth it. I got myself into a mess on drugs. I couldn't see any way out. But you aren't messed up the way I was. You still have a chance."

I thought about Joe's funeral. I knew Joe had been having a hard time. I just hadn't known how hard.

I had been mad at Joe for killing himself. I had felt like my friend had pulled a dirty trick on me.

If only Joe had talked to me about what was wrong, I would have been there for him. I could have at least tried to help him.

I wondered if Beth would feel the same way if I killed myself. Would she be mad at me?

I thought for a minute. Beth deserved more from me than this.

I put the gun down carefully. I started

to think that maybe it wasn't too late for me. Maybe I could still make it.

I just had to get out of that house. My mom and dad were driving me crazy. I had to get away from them.

I decided to see our social worker the next day. We had a new social worker. She was better than the others. Maybe she could put me in another foster home.

Maybe she could find someone for me to talk to about my problems, too. I knew I couldn't keep trying to fight my awful feelings alone.

My feelings were starting to get the best of me. I was losing control.

Joe hadn't found anybody to talk to about his drug problem. But there was still time for me.

I looked down at the gun. My feelings of despair had gone away. But I knew they would be back. Next time, I was going to have someone around who could help me sort things out.

I knew I couldn't count on Joe's face flashing before me every time I started to feel bad about myself. But that day, I thanked Joe for being there.

HOT SHOT

Rusty had been in reform school for almost a month. He seemed to attract trouble like a magnet.

A new kid walked into the classroom. Rusty casually flexed his legs, leaving his feet in the aisle. The new kid looked too late. He tumbled over Rusty's feet and landed on the floor.

Rusty laughed boisterously.

The new kid stood up and walked to a desk in the back of the room.

"I guess the kid needs to watch where he's goin'." Rusty snickered.

There was no use lying. Rusty could never lie to Miss Cavelli. He never got away with anything when she was around. She was strict and tough. The only time Rusty had any fun was when she left the room.

Miss Cavelli had been helping another new teacher. She was having a hard time with one of her kids. She asked Miss Cavelli for a hand.

Miss Cavelli had only been teaching for two years herself. She was young, too. But she never had to yell to make everybody do what she wanted. The kids listened to Miss Cavelli.

Rusty wished he was in the other teacher's class. The kids did whatever they wanted in there. The teacher had no control. She was always asking Miss Cavelli for help.

One time Miss Cavelli had sent Rusty to a big, empty room after she caught him fighting. He had sat there all alone for two hours. He had almost gone crazy. He had only managed to get through it by thinking up ways to make even more trouble.

He had come up with the perfect plan. The last time he had visited his home, Rusty had stolen his little brother's ant farm. He had brought it back to school with him.

Rusty thought he could break down Miss Cavelli. He put the ant farm in her desk and cracked the glass case.

At first it *was* fun. But Miss Cavelli just stared at him. He started to wonder if he had made a mistake.

"It's just a bunch of ants," he told her.

"All right, Rusty," Miss Cavelli said, "when I dismiss the rest of the class, make sure *you* stay right here. Is that clear?"

Rusty felt like yelling, "No, it isn't!" But he knew better. Miss Cavelli would only make him do twice as much time if he caused a scene.

After the kids left, Miss Cavelli came over to Rusty's desk. "You have an hour of time to do. Get going," she ordered.

The next hour was awful. Rusty pounded on the walls. Nobody heard him. He would have broken a window. But there were no windows in the room.

At last his time was up. He heard the last bell ring.

A few minutes later, Miss Cavelli came into the bare room. She sat down next to Rusty on the hard floor.

For a long time she didn't say anything. Her silence made Rusty nervous. He wished she would say *something*. Anything would be better than the awful silence.

He was about to ask her if he could go when she spoke.

"Rusty, I'd like to tell you some words from a poem I like very much," she began.

"I hate poems." Rusty scowled. He wasn't going to make it easy for her.

"Well, I won't tell you the whole poem," she said with a smile. She just wouldn't get mad at him. That made Rusty feel even worse. She *should* get mad. She had a right to get mad. He'd be mad if he were in her shoes.

"The words I remember go like this," she said, " 'Ah wud some power the gift e gie us, to see oursilves as ithers see us.' "

She stopped and waited. Rusty didn't say a thing.

"The poem was written by Robert Burns, a Scottish poet," Miss Cavelli told him. "He wrote it many years ago. Do you know what those words mean?"

"They don't even sound like English to me," Rusty said.

"That's because they were written in the way some people in Scotland talked back then."

"So what does it mean?" Rusty asked. He started to wonder about the strange words.

"Well, let's take the prank you pulled today."

"What has that got to do with it?"

"I think you wanted the rest of the class to notice you. You thought they would notice you if you caused trouble for me. Maybe you thought the other kids would think you were a hot shot if you goofed off."

"I didn't care what they thought," Rusty said. But he wondered how she seemed to know everything. She even knew the things she wasn't supposed to know.

"The trouble is," Miss Cavelli said, "the kids didn't see you as a cool guy. They were angry because you bothered them while they were working."

"So what?"

"So, that's what Robert Burns' poem is all about. He's saying, if only we could see ourselves the way other people see us. Most of the time we don't. But I have a way for you to get the kids to see you as a hot shot. That is, if that's what you want to be."

"Forget it," he told her.

"Okay. But if you change your mind, let me know," she said. She got up from the floor. "I don't mean the kind of hot shot that kids don't like, Rusty," she added. "Those hot shots are just show-offs. I'm talking about the kind of hot shot kids look up to."

She left before he could say another word. Rusty sat there for a few more minutes. He wondered what kind of plan she had in mind.

Nobody had ever bothered to come up with a plan for him before. He had been in one mess after another. Finally, he had ended up in this place.

The rules were strict at the reform school. It wasn't any fun. After school he had jobs to do. He had to clean some of the rooms and work in the kitchen.

At night, he had homework. There were no TV sets, or parties, or cars, like he'd been used to. He used to spend more time going to parties and running around than he had in school.

All that fun had changed after his last run-in with the law. He had been caught breaking into a store at night. He had thought he had everything planned perfectly. He never should have been caught.

But the plan didn't work. After the police had caught him in the store, his mother had said she couldn't handle him anymore. He had taken some tests. Then they had sent him to this awful place. Now he spent his days working hard in class. After school he worked on the jobs they piled on him.

Rusty had tried to get out of the place a few times. He had always been caught. After a while, he had given up. Some weekends he got to go home *if* his mom wanted to see him. Sometimes she didn't.

It was just as well. He didn't much like being home anyway. His mom nagged at him. She liked his little brother better. Why shouldn't she? His little brother didn't cause her the pain he did.

Rusty knew his mother thought he had turned out just like his old man. His old man was in jail for killing someone. Why should Rusty's mother think Rusty was any different? He had been in trouble ever since he was a little kid.

Now Miss Cavelli said she had a plan that could change all that. People wouldn't think he was a loser anymore. They would see him as one of the good guys.

Rusty shook his head. "No thanks," he said out loud. He didn't want any part of it. He got up. He was late for kitchen duty. The cook would be mad.

But while he worked in the kitchen, Rusty kept thinking about what Miss Cavelli had said. He kept wondering about her plan after he got back to his room. What kind of a plan could it be?

The next morning he woke up early. He couldn't get back to sleep. He kept wondering about the plan.

He went to his classroom early. Miss Cavelli was already there. He knew she would be. She was always there early.

"Why, Rusty," she said in surprise. "It's nice to see you on time for a change."

He slammed his books on the table. "I want to hear about your plan," he yelled.

Miss Cavelli just smiled. "I thought you might," she said quietly. "Sit down. I'll tell you."

He sat down. He wondered why he always did what Miss Cavelli asked. With anyone else, he did just what they *didn't* want.

"You know Miss Sanchez is having a lot of trouble with a few kids in her class," Miss Cavelli said.

"So?"

"So maybe you can help her out."

"Why would I want to do a thing like that?" he asked.

"If you can get those kids in shape, you'd be a real hero with all the kids in that room and in ours. You know which kids cause trouble."

"Sure. Everybody does. But they're just like me. Why should they listen to me?"

"Because you could be a leader if you wanted, Rusty," Miss Cavelli said softly.

"I don't know what you mean."

"So far you've led people to destroy things," Miss Cavelli said. "People do follow you. They have followed you to steal, to take drugs, to get into all kinds of trouble. I'd like you to use your talents as a leader to get those kids shaped up."

"I don't know why you think I can do that," Rusty said.

"Don't you think you can?" Miss Cavelli asked him.

"I — I don't know," he stammered. What was the matter with his voice? He never had any trouble talking. He was even known as a big mouth. Why was it so hard to talk now?

Miss Cavelli was putting the pressure on him. He felt all choked up. He'd better not fall apart. He'd die if he did.

But if Miss Cavelli saw that he was acting strangely, she didn't say anything about it. All she said was, "I know you're good at math, Rusty. You're a whiz at math. I'd like you to be a student teacher. I want you to spend some time in Miss Sanchez's room every day. I'd like you to work with those tough kids on their math."

"Why should they listen to me?" Rusty asked.

"Why do you listen to me?"

Rusty thought about Miss Cavelli's question. "I guess it's because I know you mean what you say. You're pretty tough yourself."

She nodded. "I'd like you to be tough when you work with those kids. I know you can get them to come around."

"Well, I guess I could give it a try."

"You'll give it more than a try, Rusty. You'll do it," she said strictly. Then she added, softly, "I know you can."

It seemed strange having somebody think he could do something decent. But Miss Cavelli thought he could do it. She must be right.

Sure she was right. She was always right. It was nice to know he was good enough in math to help others.

Not that they'd look on it as help. Not at first, anyway. They'd fight him all the way. Just like he had fought Miss Cavelli.

He gave her a big smile. "I guess if I act as mean as you, I can do it," he told her.

She smiled back at him. "You've got it, Hot Shot," she told him as she shook his hand firmly.

Hot Shot. It didn't sound too bad. This plan had to work. It might even be fun.

Besides, he had outgrown those childish pranks. If Miss Cavelli wanted him to teach math, he must be a whiz, just like she said.

He couldn't wait to get his math

lesson started.

"Excuse me, Miss Cavelli. I've got work to do," he said. He took his math book off the table. "I don't have any time to waste."

"Neither do I," Miss Cavelli shot back. She went over to her desk and got back to work.

They were tough, both of them. He knew now that she was tougher. So far, anyway. But if he could make it as a student teacher, maybe he could become just as tough.

It would be fun to be a real hot shot. This was one plan that was going to work.

THE MISSING MONEY

Randy didn't like Bob Johnson very much. Bob seemed to do better than Randy in just about everything. Bob was a better athlete. He wrote stories for the school paper. He had lots of friends. And Mrs. Clint, the math teacher, liked Bob.

But there was one thing Randy could do better than Bob. Randy got better grades. But Mrs. Clint didn't seem to notice that.

She was always hard on Randy. She made him go to the board and do math problems in front of the whole class. She called on him all the time. Randy knew she didn't like him. She was his hardest teacher.

But Mrs. Clint was nice to Bob. She never called on him. Instead, he always got to help her with the fun things. She sent him on errands. He got to go to the office for things. Mrs. Clint never let Randy run the errands.

Randy and Bob were in Mrs. Clint's class right before lunch. Every day someone got to leave early to turn in the lunch count. Everyone wanted the job.

One day Randy asked if he could take the lunch count to the office. Mrs. Clint told him that Bob was taking it.

Randy was angry. It just wasn't fair that Bob did all the fun things. Bob was Mrs. Clint's pet.

At lunch that day Bob was ahead of Randy in line. The cooks were serving ice cream bars for dessert. Randy loved ice cream bars. But Bob got the last one.

That made Randy even angrier. If only he had left class early, then he could have had an ice cream bar. But Bob got it instead. Just like Bob got everything else.

After lunch everyone went outside. Randy found Bob playing basketball with some of the guys. Randy walked up to him. "Bob, do you know what you are?" Randy asked.

Bob stared at Randy with a puzzled look on his face. He didn't know what Randy meant.

"You're a teacher's pet. That's what you are," Randy said.

"You don't know what you're talking about," Bob said. He took a shot at the basket.

"Why does Mrs. Clint let you do everything?" Randy yelled.

"I don't do everything. And anyway, why does it matter?"

Randy was getting mad again. "You do plenty. And it matters because I want to help her, too! But I have to do all the hard stuff. How come you never have to do problems on the board?"

"Listen, Randy. I just do what she asks. I'm not doing anything to you," Bob said.

"Well, why don't you quit playing up to Mrs. Clint?" Randy yelled. He grabbed Bob's jacket. He pulled Bob's face close to his own and shouted, "Then maybe someone else can do something fun for a change, Teacher's Pet!"

Bob pushed Randy away. He looked angry. Randy thought he was going to say something. But he turned around and picked up his basketball. The guys started playing again.

Randy stood there frowning. The students near him stared. Randy felt a little bad. Maybe he had looked pretty stupid yelling at Bob about being a teacher's pet. Maybe it wasn't *all* Bob's fault. But still, it wasn't fair. Bob got to do everything.

Randy turned and went inside to the study hall. Mrs. Clint supervised the study hall after lunch. Bob was in the class, too.

Randy walked into the room and sat down. As soon as Bob came in Mrs. Clint called him to her desk. She handed him something and he left the room.

Randy wanted to get out of the room, too. He walked up to Mrs. Clint's desk.

"What is it Randy?" she asked when he stopped at her desk.

"Can I go the the office, Mrs. Clint? I want to pay for my class ring." Randy had been saving his money for a long time. He really wanted that ring.

"Okay, Randy," Mrs. Clint told him. "But don't be gone too long. I want to talk to you about Bob."

So bigmouth Bob had talked to Mrs. Clint. He had told her what Randy had said about being the teacher's pet.

"I don't have anything to say," Randy said.

"Well, I do," said Mrs. Clint. Her face was stern. Randy knew he couldn't argue. He decided he might as well get it over with.

"Okay, I'll be back soon," Randy told her. "I just have to turn in my money."

There was a long line at the office. Randy was glad. He wasn't in any hurry to go back to his study hall. After a few minutes, Randy got to the front of the line. He reached into his pocket for his money.

Randy's heart stopped for a second. His money wasn't there. He checked again. The pocket was empty.

"I had my money this morning," he told the woman behind the counter. "It was in my pocket." He reached into his pocket again.

"I'm sorry you can't find your money," the woman said. "But please move out of the way. A lot of people are waiting. If you find your money, come back. Why don't you check the Lost and Found?"

Randy checked his back pockets. He wanted to be sure. But the money wasn't there, either.

Randy wondered what had happened. He knew it had been there. Someone must have taken it. Then he knew. Bob took it! He had taken it when Randy had grabbed him.

Randy ran back to the study hall. He stormed up to Bob. "What did you do with my money?" he yelled.

"What money?" Bob asked.

"Don't lie to me!" Randy shouted. He held Bob by the arms and shook him. "You know what money. It was in my pocket this morning. And now it's gone."

"That doesn't mean I took it," Bob said.

"Oh, yes it does," Randy told him. "You would do something like that. You took it when we were arguing outside today." He grabbed Bob's shirt. The pocket tore.

"Randy, stop it," Mrs. Clint said sharply. She came over to the boys. "What's wrong with you?"

"Nothing's wrong with me. It's your pet, Bob. *He's* done something wrong

81

this time," Randy told her.

"Randy, Bob isn't my pet." Mrs. Clint sighed. "Tell me what happened."

Randy told her about the missing money. But Mrs. Clint didn't seem to agree with him. Of course she took Bob's side.

"That doesn't mean that Bob took it," she said. "Are you sure you had it? Was the money in your pocket this morning?"

"Yes, I had it," he told her. "And it's gone now. Bob took it."

"You don't know that," Mrs. Clint told him. "You shouldn't accuse Bob of taking the money. You could be making a big mistake."

"You always take his side," Randy said.

"I'm not on his side. But you can't just blame him without thinking. You

don't even know your money has been stolen."

"What do you mean?" asked Bob.

"Let's think back," Mrs. Clint said. "What did you do with the money this morning, Randy?"

"I put it in my pocket," Randy told her. "And now it's gone. Bob took it."

"Slow down," Mrs. Clint said. "Did you check all of your pockets?"

"Sure. It wasn't in any of them," Randy told her.

"How about in your jacket pockets?" Mrs. Clint asked.

"No, but I know the money isn't there," Randy said.

"Let's go to your locker and check, just in case," Mrs. Clint said.

"Okay, but if it's not there I hope you'll believe that Bob took it," Randy said.

Randy, Bob, and Mrs. Clint walked quickly to Randy's locker. Randy opened it and pulled out his jacket. He reached into his pocket.

Then he felt the money. He pulled it out and looked at it. He counted it. It was all there.

Randy looked embarrassed. "Oh. I guess I did have the money," he said softly.

Mrs. Clint nodded.

"I'm glad you found it, Randy," Bob told him. "I can see why it looked like I took it."

Mrs. Clint looked at the boys. "Don't you have something to say to Bob, Randy?" she asked.

Bob was being awfully nice about the whole thing. Randy knew he wouldn't have been as calm.

"I'm sorry, Bob," Randy said.

KID BROTHER and Other Stories
Dianne Swenson

Steven's team gathered in left field. Maybe they wanted to kick Steven off the team — all because of his little brother, Scott.

But where was Scott? He wasn't by the bench or on the playground. Scott couldn't be left alone. He couldn't cross streets. Someone had to help him. What if something had happened to him?

Other stories in this book: "Gossip Gets Back," "A Day with Fish," "Lost in the Woods," and "New Girl on the Block."

THE DAY DAD CRIED and Other Stories
Dianne Swenson

Dana tried to hide her troubled homelife, but her abusive father finally went too far.

Other stories in this book: "A Problem with Mother," "A Baby Again," "The Other Woman," and "No More Chances."

"Randy, why did you accuse Bob so quickly," Mrs. Clint asked.

"Well, he always seems to get to do fun errands," Randy told her. "I don't see why you're so hard on me."

"You think I'm hard on you, Randy, I know," Mrs. Clint said. "But there's a reason. You're a good student. You just need to be pushed a little. Do you see?"

Randy looked at her. "I guess so," he said.

"You two help me in different ways," Mrs. Clint told them. "You help me in class, Randy. You help me show the class how to figure out the answers. Bob helps me, too. He runs errands for me. Bob isn't better than you, Randy. And you aren't better than Bob. You two aren't the same. Wouldn't life be boring if we were all the same?"

Randy thought about it for a second. Mrs. Clint was right. He wouldn't want all his teachers the same.

"I guess people should be different," he agreed with her.

Mrs. Clint was one step ahead of him, as usual. "Sure. Aren't you glad you have five different teachers? You wouldn't want five of me, would you?"

Randy just smiled. Maybe Mrs. Clint wasn't so bad after all. And maybe Bob was okay, too.

After all, Bob could have been mad at Randy. He had reason to be. But he wasn't. In fact, Bob was okay.

So what if Randy wasn't like Bob. Bob was Bob. And Randy was Randy. And Randy liked that.

**THE WELL-KEPT SECRET
and Other Stories
Dianne Swenson**

Dawn and Rick have been dating for several months.

Betsy, Dawn's best friend, just doesn't think Rick is good enough for Dawn.

Then she finds a way to make Dawn see the real Rick. All she has to do is expose one little secret.

Other stories in this book: "Running Last," "Going Back," "Mixed Up in the 'In' Crowd," and "Change of View."

AN ENDED FRIENDSHIP
and Other Stories
Dianne Swenson

Tim had been a powerful influence in Jo's life. He'd always been there to listen — to share his friendship.

But what had happened? Why couldn't Tim tell *her* his problems? Was suicide the only answer for Tim?

Other stories in this book: "Love Notes," "The Perfect Robot," "Under the Jacket," and "The Twins' Best Friend."

SERVING TIME AT CAMP
and Other Stories
Dianne Swenson

Walt was in trouble again. But this time it was big trouble. The judge told Walt that charges would be dropped if he would agree to be a cabin leader for troubled boys that summer.

But Walt didn't want to go to camp to help other kids. He thought he had enough problems of his own. But then Walt met Sal.

Other stories in this book: "Flunking Math," "Running the Race," "Swimming Versus the Books," and "Fire!"